## BY SAM HAMILL

### *Poetry*

Heroes of the Teton Mythos
Petroglyphs
The Calling Across Forever
The Book of Elegiac Geography
Triada
animæ
Fatal Pleasure
The Nootka Rose
Passport

### *Poetry in Translation*

Night Traveling (from Chinese)
The Lotus Lovers (from Chinese)
The Same Sea in Us All (from the Estonian of Jaan Kaplinski)
Lu Chi's *Wen Fu* (The Art of Writing)
Catullus Redivivus (Selected Poems of Catullus)
Facing the Snow: Visions of Tu Fu
Banished Immortal: Visions of Li T'ai-po

### *Essays*

At Home in the World
A Poet's Work: the Other Side of Poetry
The Poetry of Kenneth Rexroth (editor)

### *On Tape*

Blue Moves (featuring Paul Herder and Michael Phillips)
Historical Romance (music by Jon Brower)

# THE NOOTKA ROSE

To Tom –
Friend, fellow traveller

IV : 88

# THE
# Nootka
# Rose

POEMS BY

*Sam Hamill*

*BREITENBUSH BOOKS     PORTLAND*

First Printing: May 1987

2    3    4    5    6    7    8    9


LIBRARY OF CONGRESS CATALOGING-IN-PUBLICATION DATA

Hamill, Sam
    The Nootka rose.

    I. Title
PS3558.A4235N6   1987    811'.54     87-719
ISBN 0-932576-43-5
ISBN 0-932576-44-3 (pbk.)

Breitenbush Books are published for James Anderson by Breitenbush Publications, Inc. Patrick Ames, Editor-in-Chief.

Breitenbush Books, Inc., P.O. Box 02137, Portland, Oregon 97202

Designed by Tree Swenson
Composition by Walker & Swenson, Book Typographers
Cover photograph by Paul Boyer

The author and the publisher are deeply grateful to the National Endowment for the Arts, a federal agency, for a grant that helped make the publication of this book possible.

Manufactured in the USA by McNaughton & Gunn Lithographers, Inc., of Ann Arbor, Michigan.

GRATEFUL ACKNOWLEDGMENT IS MADE TO THE EDITORS OF THE FOLLOWING
PERIODICALS IN WHICH THESE POEMS FIRST APPEARED:

Anemos (a limited edition published by Matrix Press): *To Denise Levertov*
Another Chicago Magazine: *Getting It Wrong Again*
Dalmo'ma: *Conscientious Objection*
Earth First: *Oracular, On Orca Sound, Prelude*
Fine Madness: *Homage*
High Country News: *Friend*
Limberlost Press: *Paradiso Terrestre*
Luna Tack: *The Black Angel*
Pequod: *Historical Romance*
Poetry East: *A Lover's Quarrel, Naming the Beast*
Porcupine's Quil: *Friend*
The Arts (King County, Washington): *Counting the Bodies in Peacetime*
The Wilmington Review: *Her Body after All These Years*
Willow Springs: *Cloistered, "True Illumination Is Habitude," Scrutability, At Rexroth's Grave*
Zyzzyva: *Listen, Ianni*

For me, for the rose,
for the day's first light there's only one fate:
to be the music that is everywhere
heard *in* things, *as* things.

—STEPHEN BERG

# CONTENTS

# PART ONE

## CLOISTERED

It was summer on the north coast,
the wrong coast, they call it in the East.
It was summer. And summer means rain.

Rain dissolved the islands in the Sound,
it buried mountains and turned the ocean gray.
I listened to it rattle at my window.

Funny, how you wake some days
in the middle of the morning, and know
somehow a part of the world has died,

another language lifted from our tongues,
another way of knowing. And you don't know
whether the pulse you feel is yours

or is the fading beat of the world.
An eagle is not a symbol for a thing.
It was early summer or late spring,

I listened to the rain. For all
its tenderness and wealth, the earth
is often a meager gift.

But to know and not to speak
is the greatest grief. Listen.
The world flows away like a wave.

# A LOVER'S QUARREL

*after Roethke*

There are some to whom a place means nothing,
for whom the lazy zeroes
a goshawk carves across the sky
are nothing,
for whom a home is something one can buy.
I have long wanted to say,
just once before I die,
*I am home.*

When I remember the sound of my true country,
I hear winds
high up in the evergreens, the soft snore
of surf, far off, on a wintry day,
the half-garbled song of finches
darting off through alder
on a summer day.

Lust does not
fatigue the soul, I say. This wind,
these ever-
green trees, this little bird of the spirit —
this is the shape, the place of my desire. I'm free
as a fish or a stone.

       \*      \*      \*

Don't tell me
about the seasons in the East, don't talk to me
about eternal California summer.
It's enough to have

a few days naked
among three hundred kinds of rain.

In its little plastic pot on the high sill,
the African violet
grows away from the place
the sun last was, its fuzzy leaves
leaning out in little curtsies.

It, too, has had enough
of the sun. I love the sound of a storm
without thunder, the way wind
slows, trees darken, heavy clouds
rumbling so soft
you must close your eyes to listen:
then the *blotch, blotch*
of big drops
plunketing through the leaves.

*  *  *

It is difficult,
this being a stranger on earth.
Why, I've seen pilgrims come
and tear away at blackberry vines
with everything that's in them, I've seen them
heap their anger
up against a tree
and curse these swollen skies.

What's this? — a mountain beaver
no bigger than a newborn mouse
curled in my palm,
an osprey curling over tidepools and lifting
toward the trees, a wind at dusk
hollow in the hollows of the eaves,

a wind over waves
cooling little sandcrabs washed up along the beach.

Each thing, closely seen,
appears more strange
than before: the shape of my desire
is huge, vague,
full of many things
commingling –

dying bees among the dying flowers;
winter rain and the smoke it brings.
If it fills me with longing,
it is only because we are wind and smoke,
flower and bee,
it is only because
we are like the rain, falling,
falling through our own most secret being,
through a world of not-knowing.

       \*      \*      \*

At the end of the day,
I come, finally,
to myself, I return to the strange sounds of a man
who wants to speak
with stones, with the hard crust of earth.
But nothing listens.

When the sea hammers the sea-wall,
I'm dumb.
When the nighthawks bleat at dusk, I'm drunk
on the sadness of their songs.
When the moon is so close
you can almost reach it through the trees,

I'm frozen, I'm blind,
or I'm gone.

Fish, bird, stone, there's something
I can't know, but know the same:
I hear the rain inside me
only to look up
into the bitter sun.

What do we listen to, what do we think
we hear? The sound
of sea-walls crumbling,
a little bird with hunger in its song:
*You should have known! You should have known!*

           \*       \*       \*

Like any Nootka rose,
I know there are some
to whom a place is nothing. Like the wild rose,
like the tide and the day,
we come, go, or stay according to a whim.
It is enough, perhaps,
to say, *We live here.*
And let it go at that.

This wind lets go
of everything it touches.
I long to hold the wind.
I'd kiss a fish
and love a stone
and marry the winter's rain

if I could persuade this battered earth
to let me make it home.

## "TRUE ILLUMINATION IS HABITUDE"

A perfect halfmoon glistens
in the mist high over
the young bamboo.

The smoke-stained glass
I watch it through
makes a perfect halo

around it, as though
the moon were full. Below,
the trees are doubly dark

where no breeze lifts
a leaf — nothing moves
that doesn't move

toward sleep. You move,
in another room,
into the Dreamtime world,

your hair flooding out
in waves
around your face.

The night is so
perfectly still
I can hear your every breath

above my beating heart.
The fire's long since
gone out.

Alone by my lamp
I read Rexroth's
*Signature of All Things*

and once again,
like that swift bird
rising from its ashes,

the old ghost rises
from the wreckage of
this world

to touch my semi-
conscious life.
Poetry, Tu Fu says,

that will last
a thousand generations
comes only as

an unappreciated life
is passed.
I lay aside the book

and rub my weary eyes
just as Po Chu-i did
reading Yuan Chen

on his boat, by candlelight,
a thousand years ago.
I sit motionless

in the motionless night
while the mist
deepens

and the whole house
cools, and I listen
to your breath

and measure it against
this slow, insistent tolling
of our flesh.

# HOLY WEEK, 40084

The daffodil flowers have all fallen.
You turn out the lights and undress
and come to me.

Moonlight floods the window
with the lavender blossoms
of our weeping cherry tree.

# TO DENISE LEVERTOV

"I wanted to learn you by heart,"

I wanted the music of
    "your intense unmusical voice"
to carry the weight of the poem
        that carries us
toward the warm
    wet light of the hopeful:

poems
to remind us forever
    of Allende,
the way
    and reason
he died;
        or the pathetic beauty
and sadness of
    those groans men make
when a lovely woman passes –

as though they could sniff out
    the grace
of her compassion.

        *      *      *

And so I sit
    beside the woodstove, reading:
how easily I am pleased
    and how rarely! –
                the outer

warmth of the fire, the inner
    heat of the line.

Hungry
    for food as for justice,
I take the round vowels
    deep into my mouth,
my tongue
    and lips careful to arouse
each consonant between:

    that taste
    of the luminous dust.

    \*      \*      \*

And you give me and give me
that which I didn't know I had –

the bread of the knowledge
    of "suffering humanity"
we share as we carry,
    eating as we go. If

I may retrieve
    from these graces
some aspiration
    to inner joy and goodness,

shall I praise you
more highly than the Goddess?

    \*      \*      \*

My strong and willing elder sister,
    it's you and I must stand
against the murderous technicians:

    traffickers in arms
    and lives
    and wisdom; marketeers;
    all forms of theorists;
    careerists; and loathesome politicians.

In such moments of in-
    tense confrontation,
an absolute sureness
    comes over me
when the poem
    rides

    the *anemos*
    (breath or wind
    of in-
    spiration)

on which we glide
and sing.

## HOMAGE

Just because the year is ashes, we turn inside. Suddenly
Afternoon sunlight explodes through the window like
A hundred acres of wheat. (As on Christmas Eve: there were
New rosebuds on the bush beside an evergreen.

Klee would have loved them, they were so absurd.
And he would have let them fly away.
Perhaps he would have made them
Lavender instead of red, they were so regal deep
Inside themselves. But that was then.
Now there is this light which cannot be explained,
Sudden, delirious, furious light, acres of
Kernels of brilliant light, in the winter's dust,
In a century of ash and regret....

## SCRUTABILITY

Tu Fu, old and ravaged by consumption,
bent over his mulberry paper and wrote
the characters "single" and "wild goose,"
his eyes weakened by the moonlight.

Because it was October in his life,
he refilled his cup with wine.
His joys were neither large nor many.
But they were precise.

## AT REXROTH'S GRAVE

Off the bluff, white sails wind
among oil rigs pumping the Pacific.

Every grave but Rexroth's
faces toward the sea.

He faces the continent
alone, an old explorer,

hawk-eyed, sharp-tongued,
walking inland with his oar.

## PARADISO TERRESTRE

I remember the photos of Ezra Pound
by Avedon, taken twenty-five years ago;
the old poet wept profoundly at something
he'd long since forgotten. Pound's face was cracked
with age and grief, the immeasurable pain
of his learning. Wrong from the start, perhaps
he remembered Rome Radio, the anti-
Semitic cracks he snapped in anger,
what made him believe Mussolini.

Even tears can't wash away those words and wounds.
Pound wept, and he grieved, and grew silent. What hurt
hurts still, though he is ten years buried.
Memory and pain. *What thou lovest well remains.*

# PART TWO

## GETTING IT WRONG AGAIN

"…civilizations are as short-lived as weeks of our lives…."
and slowly, in the middle,
                     I close the book and lay aside
the unreal world.
                 Clouds continue to gather
overhead, outside, sliding in from the sea.
                          Nothing distinguishes them,
one from the other, but bulk or weight
                     or the pathetic tint
gray sunlight lends their hair.
                 Thus the universal
devours each particular, each life
                   reduced to its essential. What
can I know
           is not a question. Of course, I wanted power, I wanted
the power to save,
             not a civilization, but one small petal
from its blossom.
                For in its perfect hour
it was lovely. But not a week. Not even
                     one whole day – this perfect
product of ten thousand
              thousand years – perfection –
before the cleansing rain.
             Before the hand
protects the heart with its tight fist again.

# ORACULAR

Gray alders turn glistening black
in moonlight so yellow
it has blinded all the stars.

In all the leafless night,
no sound.
Rain frozen on the boughs.

# CONSCIENTIOUS OBJECTION

*As the years go by*
*the judges who condemn you grow in number;*
*as the years go by you converse with fewer voices,...*
                    – SEFERIS, "Thrush"

*human, / / word like an archway, a bridge, an altar....*
                    – LEVERTOV, "Vocation"

Those who rose up against arms so long ago rise up again
in anger, their voices strange and cold
sounding the names of Nicaragua and El Salvador
where, twenty years before, we sounded
together the names of Cambodia, Laos, and Viet Nam.

But I am dumb. Winter draws in its nets of silver.
Each day we draw more distant from the sun.
Sometimes we manage one small moment of epiphany –
a glimpse of greater harmony within –
but too soon turn back toward the winter paths we came from,

harsh in all our judgments, harsh in voice
and tone. "I will die," a poet once declared, "but that is
all that I will do for death." Like her, I too
will be counted among the living; I too stand against
the few who make a profit peddling death.

But I am numb: "When one's friends hate each other / how can there
be peace in the world?" A shard of sunlight
slicing through a cloud could never penetrate a heart
more deeply than the necessity to speak
directly, but I can't. I, too, have visited the dead.

I counted friends among them. I counted
a few that almost made me glad. Herakleitos said
the thunderbolt will rule our lives, but he
is also dead, and we are left among the monuments
to grieve. And to invent a Paradise.

   *   *   *

There is a great sea called Tranquility. I saw it once
on a map. There were white ships with white sails
blown by Adriatic breezes, there were cargoes of dream
and belief — I saw it all on the map.
But I could never take you there. I can't find it again.

But here is the sea I know, cold and hard,
bitter in its judgment, flattened by a sky of solid ash.
The day's news arrives with its nerves exposed,
and we are hardened, our blood cools, and a ghost from the past
delivers our Narcissistic sermon

in the same old monotone our parents heard at Auschwitz
or Treblinka. When summer comes, the sea
will turn to gold and we will see our reflected faces
in the water. Only then can we remember
the many-hearted rose opening, one after another,

its own most secret chambers to the end.
We walk on the ashes of the dead beneath a sky of ash.
The Japanese combine the word for word
with the word for temple to get the word for poetry.
Temple word. Holy word. No Word can save.

But we all have wounds only a few right words can poultice.
We long all winter for summer's blue,
all summer we long for quiet. The voices we converse with

year by year grow fewer. In the Temple of the Dead,
speak softly. And if you must speak, praise.

*      *      *

Those who rose in protest long ago rise up again.
I, who am brother to dragons and friend
to the hosts of the dead, have tuned my harp for mourning,
I listen for sobs in the night. Black ships
sail out on seas of solid black. Our bitter countrymen

can't hear the winds that blow, can't see the knives
that slice our hands, can't taste the salt of seas we weep forever.
Our children grow older, early, older
than we will ever be. In the true country of the heart,
the dead rise up again, they rise and sing.

But we are not the dead. This sky of ash is cold and gray
above us, the earth itself is gray.
It's January. We miss the sweet stench of flowers.
The winter sun has gone where winter suns
all go – south into the sea. The world is a cell door slammed

against our faces while we breathe the fetor
of burning human flesh that rises from our sea of need,
our ocean of desire. Someone brought me
a winter rose to lift me from my dolor. Simple gifts
overpower. Peace in El Salvador

lives in the price one pays for a single flower to give one's
friend or lover. The dead are borne in us.
We were born at Sarajevo, we were born at Yalta,
in Dresden, Hiroshima, Manhattan.
The Rabbi of Auschwitz bows, grateful for life's one altar.

33

# THE BLACK ANGEL

Spring returns to the heartland
two thousand miles from the peaceful
sea of home; the heavy snows
of a week ago have vanished
into the rich, dark earth.

I walk beside the river
talking to myself, humming
a fragment of song I thought
to decipher from Chinese,
just a little song of hurting

from a thousand years ago. A few clouds
scud past. Mallards settle on the water
or climb the banks to preen.
I stretch out on the bank,
shirt off, soaking up the sun.

Neither awake nor asleep,
I feel a heavy shadow float across
my face: and open my eyes
to wide, blue, cloudless
Iowa skies, wondering what wing

lifts me from a dream and back
into this world. And suddenly
I remember the huge wing and bent head
of the black angel who rose
over that Russian grave

in the hilltop cemetery where
I walked through falling snow

last week. But I don't
remember the name. All the same, I know
something of her grief,

that beautiful bronze body
blackened by age, her right hand
pointing not toward heaven,
but toward
unknowable wastes to the north.

Thus the spirit in its going forth
longs not for the peace of seas
or heavens, not for the orthodox
sailing out into the embrace
of angels' wings,

but for the perfect knowledge of
a single cell dying or dividing,
the intertwining hopes
and loves of days with dark soil
and frozen wastes

only the human heart can grow.
It is Third Moon, Year
of the Rat, in the most loveless
country in the most friendless
century of the world. Thus

Li Yu walked across the palace lawn alone
a thousand years ago, Ching Ming Festival
marking the end of cherry blossom time
and no place in the world
for him to bare his soul.

Thus two Russian immigrants
in frozen Iowa graves – a third

has already chiseled her first date.
Redwing blackbirds
swarm through all the trees.

Melancholy, dozing
on a beautiful spring day,
I see at last
Li Yu's old song, how
it's sung with a broken voice:

*If you want to know*
*the sum of human pain,*
*watch the soft brown river*
*rolling eastward in the spring.*

## NAMING THE BEAST

*"There are no limits to masculine egotism in ordinary life. In order to change the conditions of life we must learn to see them through the eyes of women."* —LEON TROTSKY

Woman, I return to you
                    first with my eyes
which are broken
            by their cargo like wings
of a butterfly nailed
           to a board under glass,

so beautiful and so useless —
                  I return to you
first with my eyes
           which are bleeding.
Let others talk
         about sleep, about dreams

and their meanings.
              I dream a woman
in ice and mud, freezing,
             begging
me to save her unborn baby,
                the way I clawed

and clawed to reach her
             until my nails were broken,
flesh ripped open
          on splinters of ice

and the terrible sound
                    of her breathing.

I couldn't save her.
                    But there was no baby,
no woman, no ice.
                    It was only
a nightmare, you will say,
                    but it returns

and returns
                    like ordinary memory.
I return to you
                    with my eyes because
the terror is often
                    more bearable

for us that way,
                    because the huge
hole in your heart is
                    invisible, and no one
can see how even
                    the soul returns, weeping.

                    *        *        *

"Safe," they call it.
                    "A safe." That place
to protect you
                    from his rage. Ravaged eyes
peered down from the window
                    when I brought you,

and I knew they knew
                    the fear and pain. So they

locked you away like gold
                              that belongs to
no one
          but yourself, you became

at last your own
                    real estate,
a farm and a temple,
                        to which
only you
          may hold title.


Thirty years of agony
                        are over, your life
reassembled. Call it
                      a dream if you will,
but scars
          are always real.


And now the stars
                    in your eyes
rekindle,
          little fires of the spirit
burning through the night
                            without heat,


refusing to go out,
                      lighting the far corners
of the deepest constellations
                              of your heart
with their glow:
                you are alive.

And if I cry, it is only
                    because the canary
sings more often
                    than the eagle, because
the butterfly, although
                    beautiful, is silent.


      *       *       *


Battered, you said,
                    not beaten.
You took my hand.
                    Your voice was clogged
with grief.
                    "Battered." "Beaten."


(There is a habit
                    we have of hearing
and not knowing
                    what we did not want
to know: a hum
                    of grief around us


like a boat droning
                    on the water, but
that moan is our own
                    suffering we could not name,
unspeakable agony
                    we could not name.


We are slowly
                    drowning
our own voices.
                    We are sinking.)

You took
        my hand and I wept,


I wept myself blind
                    in the street
when I saw you had
                    named the beast
and by naming,
            defeated it.

Woman, I return
                to you now
with my ears
            which are full
of your tears
            and your laughter:


neither victim
            nor executioner,
call us simply
            human.
Naming
        what matters.

# COUNTING THE BODIES IN PEACETIME

It wasn't, really, much of a body
they dredged from the muck on the river bank.
Just a small bundle of storkish bones
with a few memories of flesh still clinging.
The twenty-fifth victim.
They are counting the bodies in peacetime.

The remains they'll name
by the teeth in a month or two,
or tag the bones with numbers.
They crawl through the drizzle
on hands and knees, soaked,
sifting the soil with spoons.

And a woman? What's a woman to do
to live, each hour a terror,
the oppressive dark like foul breath
breathed across her face, the fear —
to walk alone in the evening.
Even the crime of need can't explain it.

And a man? Because he is a man,
he feels repulsion, he is ashamed.
He wants to understand, he wants
to find the beast and slay it,
but knows the beast is in
himself, angry and afraid.

The spirit shrinks.
Good, kind hands grow numb.
Light rain darkens the new earth

they dragged her body from.
We are asking the same old questions,
counting the peacetime dead.

# PART THREE

# HER BODY AFTER ALL THESE YEARS

It is always the same:
changed.
You have come in
from the long day's fields
and now,
          as the darkness
settles around you,

you remember a grove
of apple trees
shining
          in the moonlight, how
you shinnied
up the trunk

and slid out
slowly
along the limb
until you came
                    to the leaves,
how the limb
bent

just a little
as you inched
your way along,
and how you filled
your shirt
          with apples
and swung down,

dropping
onto the moonlit ground
quiet as a squirrel
so the gruff
              farmer wouldn't
wake,
        and how,
walking home along the road,

it all seemed
like a dream
                until
you polished one
on your sleeve
              and bit in
and savored it,

your tongue
startled:
so bitter,
so sweet,
so alive.

overnight, it's autumn.

A few lank strands of sunlight
dangle through the clouds.

The hawks stopped circling meadows
and moved toward trees where varmints nest

building secret places for the winter.
The days grow fainter, and shadows last forever.

I would like to sit outside today,
to drag my rocker out to the deck and sit

and listen to your stories.
I would like to sit outside in my rocker

and pour you a glass of bourbon.
See, back in that corner,

in the shadows of the cedar,
you see that small Jap maple?

It turned yellow and red last Tuesday.
Monday, it was vermilion.

I love that goddamned tree. Autumn here
is otherwise so subtle.

But good storytelling weather – cool
enough in the evening to enjoy a little fire,

a morning chill
to stir the blood to labor.

Oh, it's not the sun I worship,
but the hour. For now, sit here.

It is a kindness when
old friends can be together, quiet.

This fine October air is ours,
friend, to share. Contemplation

is both our gentlest and
our most awesome power.

## ON ORCA SOUND

First, there was the sea
                    ("immense, wine-dark,
eternal") – rolling, wave
                    after wave;
the scream of an eagle
                    or raven, the unutterable
agony of the gulls. All that beauty
                    and all that grief
together. The rain
                    made birds' feet
dancing on the roof. Standing
                    at my window
I had a gentle rhythm
                    rising
from within and without
                    while the gray world
darkened with clouds,
                    the bird-sounds
of birds without singing,
                    an empty heart
needing filling, and
                    the ancient impulse
toward song. So far
                    from home
and nothing
                    in all the world to say.
No word. Just the world
                    and me
alone. Nothing on the tongue
                    but the feel
of a soft, wet, iridescent pearl.

# PRELUDE

Stop looking at the sea for your answer.
The sea doesn't know or forget. Those far
distant puffs dancing out of the imagination
are all that's left of what we thought we knew.
That's why the loon's cry brings a shudder.
Stop looking at the water. The sea never answers.
Let winter, for a moment, take the mind.
Night and mind are full of sound. You walk
along with your hands thrust deep in your pockets,
you walk through the deep trough of winter
and the mind teeters, teeters at the abyss
of the mind. And falls, memory clutching
at everything that rushes past falling
upward, climbing toward the light growing
ever smaller, ever fainter from above.

I saw you fall. I could not reach your hand.
Because I was falling, falling beside you,
falling in love, falling out of Paradise
with my mouth full of apple and my heart
racing toward earth like a rock dropped
from an eagle's talons. I could not help.
And now it is winter. You stand looking out
at the sea, and the sea birds make you weep.
You can see where the kelp wavers like the hair
of a drowned girl. The water glints and breaks
into shards of light. Offshore, the big rigs
are sucking the world's bones. But you can't bear
to see. The birds cry, the light sails away,
and the past passes us by. Walk by the sea,
yes. But silent. Because there is nothing to say.

# UNFORGIVEN

From the sea, this sea
of green trees
appears deep blue,

a huge, gentle
tsunami
by Hokusai.

Thus we sink
into ourselves, stones
through water,

coming to rest
in the perfect calm
of the unforgiving world.

# WITH THE GIFT OF A NOOTKA ROSE

The trill of thrushes, almost unnoticed,
there, at the edge of deepening shadows
in the shrubbery,
sadly,
and the last Nootka roses,
once bright, their pink blossoms fading
slowly in the sun,
"have the look of flowers that are looked at."

And there's a wilting in us,
a draining away like color from wild roses,
a little song
like the three pathetic notes
a robin drops from the topmost boughs of cedar.

I cannot understand
how the shape of a flower can break
a heart in two,
or how a robin on a summer day
can take my breath away.

Do you remember, years ago,
you brought me a small white
tightly shuttered rose
in a small white vase
with a single spray
of baby tears. We had quarreled, perhaps,
I had said something ugly,
and you brought me,
you said,
a rose. In lieu of an olive bough.

And now, remembering, the sun
straight and high and still, and the singular self
moving on, westward
toward the last mountains
settling into the sea, north toward the cold
white emptiness of knowing –
the self is constantly moving.

And now, years later, the beautiful
white blossoms
of ocean spray
turn dingy summer yellow.

I'd sooner give my heart to ocean spray
or to this nootka rose
than to any American Beauty. I want to
bring you this wild rose to remind you of the rose
you brought me
so long ago
a time when I had hurt you.

But surely it will die
before I can get it home.
So here I sit, lonely on a dusty summer trail
dying from the inside out,
strangling on my own heart's own in-
articulate tongue.
Drowning in my own language.

     *     *     *

For days it has hung
over everything, this emptiness, this
sweltering thing

that drains the color from our words
and lends them a useless ring,

this clammy hand
damaging my sleep. No wind
to trouble the summer's dust. A plump
garden spider builds her bridge
from thistle to thistle
where she will nest. Long-suffering thrushes
slip from shadow to shadow
through the trees. The finches get drunk on their singing.

Sometimes we are blown
like dry husks. Sometimes we can remember
only that the moon is salt and dead.

If I came to you now, we would place
our silence between us on the table
like cold gruel, our bread
and our water,
until even the night wouldn't heal us.

For the gift of a Nootka rose,
I would get on my knees
and beg
if only I knew how. But dust
has settled the summer. You brought
me a rose when I hurt you.
I loved you
when I was still a child.

           *       *       *

And now, evening coming on,
last light

sailing slowly out to sea, last birds
grown quiet,
vanishing into the trees, the sky
blue-purple and
the first stars
drifting over hills from the east,

I strip my last cigarette
and get up from this rotting stump
I've perched on half my life, it seems,
and start back home
with a fading rose in my pocket.

My shadow lies splayed
behind me like my past.
Not a sound in all the world. Even the gulls
have gone, and the shadows of trees
fall over our house
like huge, lonely hands.

Beside the incense burner
I lay a dying Nootka rose
and light a cone of musk.

A spider's thread of smoke
curls up
through the open empty hands
of Kuan Shih Yin:

bodhisattva of compassion,
goddess of mercy,
deliver us.

# Part Five

# SEPTEMBER SOWING

There are no birds and no flowers. The juncos have gone
into the heavy air of September, the robins
vanished into wet trees and falling leaves, and even the gulls
have grown silent, turning toward the sea.

Only yesterday, there were forget-me-nots, small and blue
and impossibly good to see. There was clover blossoming under bees,
scotchbroom yellow as the sun, and wild blackberries
turning dark from purple in the heat.

Now, even the ravens have flown, and the sky is gray
and hard. While the rain streaks my window,
I sit with my morning coffee and my cigarette, thinking how,
when weather's good, I harvest the fruits of the dead,

the way I remember Roethke, whom I never met,
down among the tidepools on his hands and knees
examining the barncacles on rocks, the small shells the sea
scatters along the beach. The way I remember Seferis,

whose language I couldn't even speak, the way he'd see
the garden of a sleepy Arab house changing shape
and know it as a single note in a symphony, a fragment
of song too large for any one man to sing.

The first autumn rains make a tomb of every house,
erasing bird, beast, and flower alike,
writing "emptiness" across the worn slate sky
of winter. Like an old wound that has healed

poorly, and aches when the weather changes.
The recent dead remain with us, but

their voices can't be distinguished from the cries
of those still dying. The old ones speak out singly.

Now, with the rain still falling, and my cigarette burnt out
and my coffee cold in its cup, and the small garden
turning dark, I think I can hear them again, faintly,
beyond the trees, beyond the cemetery stones,

beyond the clatter we set up to protect our ears
from the whispers of the dead. We live between the mountains
and the sea, between the music of the dead
and our own cacophony, between our own small fears

and our huge collective dread. The garden
will rise up out of the sea.
The sky will warm and clear. And we will suddenly believe
our dreams and lives are one,

that we are here just once,
if only for a moment, but we are here,
drawing our lives and language from the dead,
living our deaths together.

*    *    *

Rain. Slowly, steadily, all the long morning,
then falling mist in a heavy haze out on the water,
the western mountains a watercolor
the mist will too soon wash away. And only then,

late in the day, the sun breaks through
a crack in drifting clouds, the low plaintive wail
of sea-horns off in the Sound, and the sudden
gull-cry, shrill and lonely, slicing

the soft gray autumn sky. With the sun
slipping into the trees, our little Japanese garden
takes on a shadowy yellow glow, budding groves
of three-foot-high bamboo

looking strong, shining for the very first time
since early April. I draw a breath, slowly,
like drawing water from a well,
and the sun is gone, drowned, its last fingertips

lingering in the treetops, the earth below
returned to rich greens and shadows,
black to gray. And what is a life, and what
have I done, and what, after all, is a day?

A broken line of geese, black and silent,
wavering southward down the sky,
a brush-stroke reminding me of old Tu
"adrift between earth and heaven," his eyes

forever rising from earth to horizon
or dropping from the wide heights of heaven
to the skyline. A day in September
every September for the last twelve hundred years.

That kind old Chinese gentleman would understand,
he himself looking back at least that far again:
the same winds blowing in from the sea,
blowing yang, then yin,

the same lonely gulls wandering over tides –
you can hear them call and call again.
Age-old cedars creak and bend
as they have done since time began.

The same worn clouds overhead. The same sun.
But it is only a day in a life, you will say,
more a footnote than a song.
But the same winter comes.

\*　　　\*　　　\*

Every September dawn and dusk is like
the twilight of the world.
Praise the autumn evening: the dark
will be truly dark.

Not like in the city where the artificial twilight
lasts forever, not like the city's
infinite hum and strings of lonely lights
burning alone in the shadows

where true darkness never comes.
When the last light pales in the west, there is
neither the fear nor the sadness,
only the memory of a mild September day

as a way of knowing, a kind of learning
through mnemonics, memorizing the rhythm of the day
and of the tide and of the seasons.
It is a way of sowing fields left fallow in the mind.

Here, waiting alone in failing light,
I realize that for most of America
it is already night. Venus stirs in the west.
Soon, I will see Kueh Hsing

hiding in the Dipper. The stars the old Chinese
called Cowboy and Weaving Girl
will soon enjoy their annual reunion
high over the Yangtze River.

Blue seawater fills our veins, and stars float there
forever in the tradewinds of the heart.
Here on the edge of the floating world
I scratch out a kind of life

from rich soil and stone piled thin
on a ridge of basalt rising from the ocean.
The winter winds blow in from China and Japan.
I think the sky must be clearing.

They tell me everything grows simple
toward the end. I've wasted forty years
watching nothing out of windows, and I can't pretend:
whatever it was I've done, I did it, finally,

wrong – wanting perhaps not something
as simple as a song, I tried to join my voice
to others, but they all sang alone. I wanted
to marry my voice to a chorus,

but this life cannot be made into a scene
from old Euripedes. I feel my daughter
swimming through my blood against a tide
as certain as the sea's. By the time

she reaches me, I'm gone. She, too, will listen
to hypnotic witcheries on the wind; she, too,
will listen to the dead
and learn her song.

\*     \*     \*

Child I tore from a dream and wrenched into this world,
my only blood of my blood, I adore you.
And never so much as now.
Here where we walk the path of rain and wind,

we listen to the dialogue between the Antiphonist
and Mary of the Clouds, you with your blue beads
from Pandrosou Street and your many earrings, I
listening for the breath, the heart, for any sign

of tenderness, both of us remembering
the islands of plane trees and pine trees
and olive groves, or the great harbor at Rodos
the Colossus carefully guarded

until he fell, mortal, into the blue Ægean Sea.
We, too, will fall in time. But for now,
with night coming on, with its arms full of stars
and memories, there are the old night-sounds

we name but cannot know, the dizzying whirl
of the heavens high overhead, the soft human noises
muttered by the lonely as they turn, alone,
toward bed.

It is finally dark. Our little garden closes
in the last hint of light, shadows drowning in shadows,
wild roses and vine maple and English ivy
and thick, dense salal all turning

into a rich quilt of black brocade as I speak.
There are no birds and no flowers,
only that sweet nostalgia for summer clover
blossoming with bees.

Alive, we harvest the fruits of the dead
together, our hearts changing shape,
growing smaller or larger, forever threatening
to break.

And what is a life? And what is a day?
An old man's loneliness which can't be shared,
a young woman's work and dreams,
and a spark of light between them.

The things we've seen, we never came to know.
And those we know, we never truly see.
September swells the tides. *Gloriæ! Gloriæ!*
A poor man's life is metaphor.

## VENUS ASCENDING

You have come this far,
                    and now the blue Ægean
stretches level to the sky.
                    You have come this far
to listen to the silence of the dead,
                    to find a stone
buried at Thermopolæ,
                    to weather out the tempest
days have built into years,
                    years into something
deep beneath your grasp.
                    Now you pass
under the soft gray domes
                    of olive trees
where the gray birds
                    all are questions
you haven't the language
                    to ask. The dust
dances up around your knees
                    and swirls
through the pomegranate trees
                    and settles
over unnamed flowers,
                    lavender or jasmine,
blooming in the moonlight,
                    filling the taverna
with nostalgia and perfume.


You who were not given
                    the Greek heart or tongue,
nor the five thousand

years of her struggle,
nor her islomania
nor her gods and furies —
you are given Venus
ascending an hour before dawn,
huge and lonely, pulsing
in the skies above Turkistan,
calling through the gates of sleep,
"Come in, come in,"
but even then
you couldn't touch the sea
where it lifts the hem of sky
no matter how you tried.
You came this far
to find an oar upright in the sand.
You were anchored in a land
where words meant nothing
and nothing
was what it seemed. Venus
ascends alone over Turkistan.
You rise alone
in Faliraki.
Learning the names of things.
You needn't be Greek to be Hellene.

# A PHOTOGRAPH OF K. P. KAVAFIS

Kavafis wears a dark, striped suit. He is seated
at the end of a couch, uncomfortably, his knees
together, his heavy, ankle-high shoes placed carefully
on the floor before him like two objects, one
forearm thrown over his lap like an afterthought,

his eyes looking into the floor just beyond his feet,
the lids heavy, sagging as if from the weight
of history's ghosts. His jaw is set, his lips pursed sadly.
Behind him on the wall, a Ming tapestry tells
the story of a once-great prince, and of the love he lost.

# CLASSICAL TRAGEDY

As long as the day lasts, it will not last
long enough. The legions of the rain
ride forward in their chariots, the dark comes on.
Still, there is time enough for the sun
to light the bare brown shoulders of the girl
glancing back down a country road,
time for the click, the buzz and hum,
of summer insects in her hair.

Lying in the sun with the tragedies of Iphigenia
and Antigone, the day will not last long enough
for me to understand the breezes
in the trees or the clouds above. Sometimes
a robin sings. But when it rains,
we lift our faces up, remembering the sun
that turned our world to dust.
As if we expected the day, for a moment, to remember us.

## PSYCHE AND EROS

She climbed the dark side of the granite monolith
while Aegean sunlight climbed the other.
She was a deep silhouette rising through shadow
as the shadow grew deeper and smaller.

I watched from our rooftop, hanging out the laundry
over a whitewashed alley in Lindos
a lifetime or two ago. From down the hill
I could hear the donkeys bray.

I stretched out naked in the sun with my
battered Herodotus. She and the sun
both climbed. And she emerged
as I had dreamed her: transparent black

in blinding light among the ruins
in the Temple of Lindean Athene.

## LISTEN, IANNI

"We *are* ruled by thunderbolts,"
                              as Herakleitos said.
All night thunderbolts
                              rumbled over the Ægean,
thunderbolts lighting the sky
                              high over the crumbling temple
of Lindean Athene. Now
                              in the gray afternoon, rain
still falls as though
                              it could wash away October.
Listen, Ianni, to water
                              running through the streets,
how it adores the flat,
                              worn stones we've exhausted
with the centuries
                              of our walking. The gods
have all vanished.
                              And still we search for Helen.


To east or west,
                              the old news remains new:
death in Grenada,
                              death in Kypros, death in Lebanon,
and we pause to honor
                              Okhi Day when the Greeks
said No to the Axis.
                              Because it is better to die
than to live without a life.
                              And we say No again
because someone didn't listen,
                              because someone

needs a martyr, because
               the saints, like the gods,
are dead. Because tomorrow
               after the rain
has washed away our shame,
               we'll have to begin again
to build a simple
               home for Helen.


Wherever we go,
               we walk on the faces of the dead.
The old women dress
               in black to mourn
their dying Christ.
               Everything gets ground
into stars and stories,
               the day's birth and death,
the love all children have
               that we can't take away.
Listen, Ianni, let me
               fill your glass. The world
will too soon pass us by.
               Be still. Listen
to the sweet, sweet
               Mediterranean rain
dripping through the leaves of the pomegranate tree.

# PART FOUR

# HISTORICAL ROMANCE

I. *Alis Ubbo*

Hard rain pummels the Avenida da Liberdade.
The Rio Tejo is swollen
dark with silt and new hillside soil.
This same rain fell on the Phœnicians
who called this
Delightful Little Port
so many hundreds of years ago.

Even the beggars in the Praça do Rossio
have clothed their twisted limbs
and gone wherever beggars go.

We walk beside the Fountain of Maximilian,
rounding the square,
three of us arm in arm,
unaware that by morning
the Algarve would be closed,
the Costa Verde
a veritable island,
all the bridges north and south
swept away downstream or out into the Atlantic.

Perched on its topmost hill
and growing darker by the hour,
the old gray stone Alfama,
eight stony centuries of blood
blackening its towers. We climb
the high walls and walk
its perimeter together,

77

pausing to search the city
from dank parapets at its corners.

Nothing but poor, black-shawled women
hanging out their laundry in the alleyways
of tenements,
nothing but a few old men with canes
and memories of war,
nothing but a few dirty children
throwing stones at alleycats or running through the rain.
Nothing changed in eight hundred years
but the bare-bulb glow of shabby rooms
one afternoon in autumn.

The same bread soup bubbles on a stove.
The same streets reek of fish and urine.
The same gray light stains everything
it touches, rich and poor alike.

A few swallows sail in the rain
over black slate roofs
as they did over Moors and Romans.
Barges and boats float slowly
down the huge brown river, round the bend,
and vanish.

We who have traveled across centuries
from a world we think is new
think this poverty is nostalgia,
that we don't belong to it.
My daughter speaks to them by name
and tells them about Brazil.
Because it is far away,
they think it must be better.

And we go back through evening light
and heavy rain,
back to our hotel to drink alone in the bar.
My daughter takes my face in her hands
and holds it like a mother.
And says,
Don't worry,
tomorrow we'll take the train
to Evora, it's the only line that's left.

And my partner says,
And if that's not enough,
we can ride the bus all day
in hard-backed seats
to take in a *juerga* in Seville,
we can visit the Moorish gardens in the Alcazar,
and search the bookstalls Saturday
for Spanish editions
of Lorca and Alberti.

And if it's literary history you crave,
we'll take a single yellow rose
to throw into the river
for all the Spanish poets
who haven't any graves.

II. *Capela dos Ossos, Evora*

*"Laborare est orare."*
Saint Francis, forgive them.
How can they know what they do?
Pillars of skulls, walls of human bones,
and in your name, they pray.

And when I asked the old priest I'd spoken with on the street
how the chapel came to be built,
he pretended he didn't speak English;
and when my daughter asked in pure clear Portuguese,
he said he didn't know.

We stood inside a whole afternoon
in a silence heavy as a syrup, the bones of the fearful
or of the unafraid
five hundred years in their plaster, five hundred years,
and the terror they promise is eternal.

Outside the rain continued to fall.
Someone came in, knelt before the little altar,
and lit a single candle.
Being pantheist and pagan,
we knew it was time to go.

All night, hammer-blows of rain
rang on the cobblestones.
Cold in the Spanish dark,
I screamed myself awake,
dreams of fire and bones and blood

shattering my sleep.
To the south and the west there are seas,
calm beaches with gentle
evening breezes in the olive groves,
a history of so long ago it seems

almost like mercy, a pain so remote
we think we can embrace it,
naming it History, or Hellenism, or Love.
I cannot sleep.
"Labor is prayer,"

Tree repeats, and says a chapel built of bones
is a natural thing.
"The temple," she says,
"is neither in the bones nor of them;
they are the instrument through which it sings."


III. *Plaza de España, Sevilla*

Riding all day on a cold bus through broken fields
and hills of wild flowers,
past the relics of failed rancheros,
there were birds we couldn't name
slumping down gray skies
above huge, black Andalusian bulls
standing aloof and dark,
watching nothing, like sullen, indifferent gods
about to embrace their wounds.

And then, evening coming on and the first glimmer
of sunlight in a week,
rolling down from easy hills, the city lights
soft in the east like sunrise,
the city before us like a postcard from the true country
of a dream: huge cathedral black against the sky,
its belltower lit from below
like a masked face on Halloween
with a candle beneath the chin
to frighten all the children.

We eat gazpacho and chorizo and wander the city streets
like any good *turista*. The Torre del Oro
rises dark and shining
from the banks of the Guadalquivir,
and everywhere, we think,
we hear music. And I want,

suddenly,
to learn the names of all the flowers in Spanish,
I want to visit
my ancestor's grave in Venice,
to bring him a defeated rose from Spain.

Turning back
down narrow corridors leading toward our room,
our feet, unaccustomed to cobblestone,
ache and ache. And something else,
inside,
cold and hard
like a stone inside the heart. But just before
I fall asleep, I think: Sevilla, Sevilla,
and call it softly, feeling with my mouth –
"*Sevilla,… Sevilla,…*"
thinking it harsh and beautiful, beautiful and harsh
like love.

\*      \*      \*

Dawn arrives with its wagonload of gold –
a clatter in the street below,
and yellow sun so bright
even fine gauze curtains
can't protect my eyes.

The night's waves washed over me
and carried me out again to dream:
a memory of music in the hills,
distant music and bawling sheep,
an old man with stubble on his chin
remembering the guns,
the black boots

of the Generalissimo
on the plaza, forty-five years ago.

Walking in the warm December sun
between two lovely women, why do I remember
only dreams of martyrs,
our unaccountable failures,

our national greed?
The great cathedral built on the wreckage of a mosque
tolls the morning hour:
nine o'clock.

By ten, we're in the plaza:
the river, still and blue,
curls slowly under bridges
along the colonnade.

We walk along
looking at the coats-of-arms,
remembering what we can
of the failed revolution,
till we come
to the Capitania General —
two military guards with burp-guns
stand outside the hall.
The first steps forward
and waves us on our way.
His eyes are dead.

Beyond the river, in the Parque
de Maria Luisa,
there are jasmine and rose-trees,
narrow lanes among the fountains,
and a monument to the poet, Gustavo Adolfo Becquer, complete

with Cupid and swooning girls —
the dream of a past before the past we see.

Soon, we will fly all night
in a drone above the Atlantic.
We will bring back everything
we were given.

Who has heard the sound of boot-heels echo
on the flesh-colored tile of the plaza

will remember. And remember roses
in December
purchased from a pushcart in the plaza,

and the myrtle labyrinth
and infinite corridors
of the Alcazar.

It is autumn in a city we have dreamed.

The maple leaves are turning red, the nights
grow long and cold.

We will fly west until we vanish in the sun.

It is beautiful and sad

the way we, dying,

make monuments of the dead.